D0208856

Becoming Jane

SARAH WILLIAMS and KEVIN HOOD

Level 3

Retold by Paola Trimarco
Series Editors: Andy Hopkins and Jocelyn Potter

Pearson Education Limited
Edinburgh Gate, Harlow,
Essex CM20 2JE, England
and Associated Companies throughout the world.

ISBN: 978-1-4058-6767-2

This edition first published by Pearson Education Ltd 2008

5

Set in 11/14pt Bembo
Printed in China
SWTC/05

The authors have asserted their moral rights in accordance with the
Copyright Designs and Patents Act 1988

Produced for the Publishers by
Ken Vail Graphic Design

Published by Pearson Education Ltd

For a complete list of the titles available in the Pearson English Readers series, please
visit www.pearsonenglishreaders.com. Alternatively, write to your local Pearson Education
office or to Pearson English Readers Marketing Department, Pearson Education,
Edinburgh Gate, Harlow, Essex CM20 2JE, England.

Contents

Introduction

'His money will not buy me!' Jane said crossly.
'What will buy you?' Eliza asked, laughing at her young cousin.
Jane smiled at Eliza, but did not answer. Then she became serious
again, as she thought about her future.

This story begins in 1796 in Hampshire, the area of England where the writer Jane Austen grew up with her six brothers and her sister Cassandra. Her family did not have much money and her parents wanted her to marry a rich, important man. But Jane wanted to marry a different man – someone she loved.

Becoming Jane is a story from a film of the same name. We do not know much about Jane's early life. We can only imagine what happened to her. But people in this story are real.

Jane started writing when she was a child. But her first book, *Sense and Sensibility*, did not come out until she was thirty-six years old. This was soon followed by *Pride and Prejudice*, her most famous book.

Jane Austen is one of the world's most popular writers. Her books are enjoyed for their amusing characters and their interesting romantic stories about life in England in the late 1700s and early 1800s. All the stories have also been made into films and television programmes – some of them many times.

It was her dream to be a writer.

Chapter 1 Sunday in the Country

At the age of twenty, Jane was still living with her family in the small country village where her father was the rector. The house was not large, and the Austens did not have much money, but this was home.

One warm Sunday morning in spring, Jane, a beautiful woman with large brown eyes and wavy brown hair, was waiting for the rest of the family to get up. Bored, she started playing the piano. Upstairs, her older sister Cassandra was woken by the sound of the music and looked across the room to Jane's empty bed. In the next room, her cousin Eliza lifted her eyes from her book and smiled.

Mrs Austen, Jane's mother, tried and failed to continue sleeping.

'Jane!' she called angrily, and then turned to Mr Austen. 'That girl needs a husband!'

Robert Fowle heard Mrs Austen's shout and ran out of the small guestroom. He stopped suddenly as he found himself face to face with Cassandra, his future wife, in her nightdress. The two young people quickly turned away and returned to their rooms. Cassandra closed her bedroom door with a playful look on her face.

Downstairs, Jane had an idea, stopped playing and reached for her notebook. It was her dream to be a writer. She wrote, 'She always did as she was told. But she was not pleased ...'

◆

Later that morning, after church, the Austens made a visit to their rich, aristocratic neighbour, Lady Gresham. They stood around in the large, cold sitting-room as Mr Austen introduced their visitors to the old woman. Lady Gresham sat comfortably on her sofa, holding a warm cup of tea.

'Lady Gresham,' Mr Austen said. 'This is our cousin Eliza – the Comtesse★ de Feuillide.'

Lady Gresham looked at the young woman, unsmiling. 'Your husband is not with you?' she asked.

'My husband cannot be here,' Eliza replied coldly. 'He was killed in France.'

'Your nephew is visiting again, I see,' Mrs Austen said quickly, turning to the young man at Lady Gresham's side. 'Mr Wisley.'

Mr Wisley bowed politely.

'And this is Mr Fowle,' continued Mr Austen to Lady Gresham. 'He is going to marry Cassandra.'

'And when will you marry?' Lady Gresham asked Cassandra.

'Not for some time,' Cassandra said softly.

'Why not?'

Robert spoke. 'I must first go to the West Indies. I will marry Cassandra when I return.'

'I see,' said Lady Gresham coldly, as she started to drink her tea.

The Austens stood and watched Lady Gresham. The room grew uncomfortable with the silence.

'Mr Wisley,' said Mrs Austen in a loud voice. 'Jane likes dancing and the Basingstoke Dance will be soon.'

Jane looked at her mother angrily, with wide eyes. Mr Wisley turned to Jane and smiled, but she looked away. Mr Wisley was very tall, but not handsome. Jane knew that he did not like talking about flowers or trees or books. These were her interests, but not his. In Jane's eyes, he was ordinary – not the type of man she could ever love deeply.

'My nephew does not enjoy dancing,' the old woman said.

★ Comtesse: a French word for the wife of an aristrocratic Frenchman

Mr Wisley was very tall, but not handsome.

'I see,' said Jane. 'That is a pity, as these dances are very important to life here in the country. They are places where young people can have pleasant conversations.'

Mr Wisley looked embarrassed. He said simply, 'Then I shall go to this dance.'

After the uncomfortable visit ended, the Austens walked away from Lady Gresham's large house. As they crossed the old woman's land, Jane's mother spoke angrily to her daughter.

'Jane, how could you be so rude to Mr Wisley? He is an unmarried man – and an important one.'

'Mother, please,' Jane said, moving away from her.

'You know our situation!' her mother continued. 'And Mr Wisley is Lady Gresham's favourite nephew. He already has the land *and* money that his father left him. But he will have a lot more in the future.'

Mrs Austen looked out hopefully at the hills, trees and lakes that were all on Lady Gresham's land.

Jane walked faster away from her mother and joined Eliza.

'His money will not buy me!' she said crossly.

'What *will* buy you?' Eliza asked, laughing at her young cousin.

Jane smiled at Eliza, but did not answer. Then she became serious again, as she thought about her future.

Chapter 2 City Life

At a men's club in London, the rooms were crowded and noisy. In every room people were drinking and having loud conversations. In one smoky room, a group of people stood in a circle and watched two men boxing. Tom Lefroy, a handsome young man, was one of the boxers. He was quick as he moved around his teacher. He was hitting the other man hard with his strong arms – but not hard enough.

His friend Henry Austen, Jane's older brother, came into the room. That night he was wearing his bright red coat because he was returning from his duties as a soldier.

'Lefroy!' Henry called out.

When he heard Henry's voice, Tom turned his head. He was immediately hit in the face, and fell hard on to the floor. Quickly, a woman hurried across the room and offered him a glass of wine. Then she helped him to get up. He smiled at her and she kissed him on the side of his face. She worked at the club and knew him well.

'Winning again, I see,' said Henry, walking up to Tom. The two friends laughed and shook hands.

'So, how long will it be before you return to the country?' asked Tom.

'A day,' Henry said sadly. 'I would like to stay here, but I have not got enough money.'

'Poor Henry,' Tom said jokingly.

'Henry!' called a shaky voice from the other side of the room.

It was John Warren, another friend of Henry's. He was standing nervously against a wall. A strange woman stood in front of him, touching his suit and then his hair. Her interest was clearly making him very uncomfortable.

Henry and Tom pushed their way around people to reach him.

'Mr Tom Lefroy,' Henry said, 'let me introduce you to Mr John Warren. John is going to go to Hampshire with me tomorrow. My father is going to prepare us both for positions in the Church.'

'Really?' Tom said, shaking hands with John.

'I understand that you have visited Hampshire, Mr Lefroy,' John said. 'Was it a long visit?'

'Very long,' Tom said with a smile. 'Almost three hours.'

After Tom changed his clothes, the three men went out together to a bar. They continued to drink and talk.

♦

The following day, Tom was tired and his head hurt from his late night. But he was a law student and he often had to go to courtrooms and make notes.

That day his uncle, Judge Langlois, was sitting in the judge's seat. When Tom arrived late, his uncle's long, grey face gave him a serious look.

The judge then turned back to a poor man in dirty clothes, and continued to speak. The man was in court for stealing pigs. He was clearly afraid of Judge Langlois.

'You and people like you are a danger to all honest, hard-working people,' Tom's uncle said. 'You have no place in our world.'

He sent the man away to Australia for the rest of his life.

After leaving the courtroom, Tom had to meet the judge in his office. His uncle, not for the first time, was unhappy with his nephew.

'Why are you in London, Tom?' he asked, taking off his coat.

'To learn the law, Uncle,' Tom said bravely.

The judge looked at him with narrow eyes. 'And to prove yourself to me. You do *want* my money after my death? I was born rich and I've stayed rich. Why? Because I follow the rules of good, honest people. I have a good reputation and I have manners.'

Tom listened in silence, feeling like a child.

'But you seem to spend your time in clubs and bars. You are drinking and boxing and spending time with the wrong kind of women,' the judge continued. 'What kind of lawyer will that make you?'

'I have a good reputation and I have manners.'

'No different from other lawyers,' Tom said with a small smile.

'It is easy to be amusing,' the judge said. 'But it is harder to be accepted in today's world.'

'But Uncle —'

'Look at your family. My sister, your mother, lost everything because she married the wrong man.'

This made Tom angry. 'She married my father because she loved him.'

'And now she is poor, and cannot look after all your brothers and sisters.' His uncle gave him a cold look. 'Who is going to do that?'

Tom tried to stay calm. 'I am, sir,' he said quietly.

'I think you need to learn a lesson, Tom,' Judge Langlois continued, more kindly. 'I am sending you to the country, to Hampshire, to be with your other relatives for the summer.'

'The country?' Tom's face showed his unhappiness.

'It will be good for you,' his uncle said. 'You must get away from London. London is full of the wrong kinds of people — people that a young man should not be with.'

'But Uncle, please,' Tom said. 'I hate the country.'

Chapter 3 A Visit from Mr Wisley

Back in the country, Jane was writing at a table, while Cassandra and Eliza were getting dressed for the evening. Guests were invited because Henry was coming home.

The two older women wanted to look their best and were excited about that evening. Cassandra asked Jane for help and her younger sister carefully tied Cassandra's hair on top of her head.

When the two sisters looked into the mirror together, Eliza

said, 'I think you two are the prettiest girls in England.'

Jane and Cassandra laughed.

Eliza continued, 'Mr Fowle will agree with me.'

Cassandra stopped laughing. 'Soon he will be far away and he will forget about me,' she said sadly.

'Impossible,' said Jane, putting her arms around her sister. 'His heart will stop when he sees you this evening.'

Cassandra smiled hopefully, but she was still worried.

Jane suddenly had an idea and hurried back to the table. She started writing again.

The other two women watched Jane. Her fingers were covered with ink. Cassandra shook her head.

'You will drive the unmarried men away with those fingers,' Eliza said.

Jane replied, 'The unmarried men can all do as they please.'

But she did not believe what she said. She knew she had to get married. It was a duty to her family.

Suddenly, there was a knock at the front door. The three young women ran to the window. From the first floor, Jane looked down on the top of Mr Wisley's head. She stepped back quickly.

But soon Jane was pushed out of the rectory and the door was closed quickly behind her. She was trying to get back inside when she heard Mr Wisley's voice.

'Miss Austen.'

She knew that her mother was watching her from inside the house. She had to talk to the man.

They walked slowly together in the garden. Mr Wisley seemed to be deep in thought and Jane was nervously searching for an idea for conversation. Finally, he spoke.

'A fine day.'

'Yes, it is,' Jane said.

'The flowers are ...' he continued, but then stopped. He

looked embarrassed and was acting strangely. Jane knew that he wanted to say something important. But she did not want to hear it.

He coughed a few times and finally spoke more decisively. 'Miss Austen, you are an interesting young lady, you are exciting and so full of life.'

Jane did not know what to say. She looked around uncomfortably, searching for an escape. Then she suddenly noticed two horses pulling a coach. They were coming towards the rectory.

'Miss Austen …' Mr Wisley continued.

'My brother!' Jane shouted.

'Who?' asked Mr Wisley

'Please excuse me, Mr Wisley,' she shouted, running to the coach with a wide smile on her face.

Mr Wisley watched Jane and called to her, 'Perhaps I could see you later?'

But Jane, of course, did not hear him.

Chapter 4 A Special Evening

That evening at the rectory, the sitting-room was filled with family, friends and neighbours. Everyone was talking and enjoying themselves. Henry was telling stories about the life of a soldier and the guests around him were laughing.

Eliza, watching Henry, said to Jane, 'I forgot that your brother was so likeable.'

'Yes, everyone admires Henry – Henry more than anyone,' Jane said with a smile. 'Everyone except me.'

The Lefroys, the Austens' neighbours, came into the room, and walked towards Jane and Eliza.

'My cousin is staying with us for the summer. He has come

from London,' Lucy said, excitedly. She was the Lefroy's fifteen-year-old daughter. 'And he is a clever young lawyer,' she added.

'Lucy, please,' said Mrs Lefroy.

But Lucy continued, 'And he has a reputation.'

'For being late?' Jane asked jokingly.

The talking and laughing in the room stopped when Mr Austen coughed loudly. He started to speak to his guests.

'Friends, neighbours – welcome,' he said. 'A family is always moving. First, our son Henry has proudly protected his country and finished his duties. Now he has returned to us with his friend John.' Mr Warren bowed to the other guests, and Mr Austen continued with his speech. 'Soon, our daughter Cassandra will leave us for a short time. She is going to help her brother Edward and his wife Elizabeth with the birth of their child.'

The guests clapped at the good news and Mrs Austen looked very proud.

'While Cassandra is away, Mr Robert Fowle will travel to the West Indies,' Mr Austen continued. 'And when he returns, he and Cassandra will marry.'

Everyone clapped again. Then they held up their glasses of wine and drank to Cassandra and Robert. The two young people smiled sadly at each other. They did not want to wait for marriage and they did not want to live in different countries for so long.

When Mr Austen's speech was finished, Mrs Austen moved around the room. She talked excitedly to her guests about Cassandra's future. John walked across the room to Jane. He was always nervous when he spoke to a woman. But he tried his best with Jane.

'Miss Austen, I understand that you are going to read one of your stories for us tonight,' he said softly.

Soon, everyone was listening to Jane as she read to them from her notebook. She told them a story about two young people who had to wait for their marriage. Everyone knew that it was about Cassandra and her future husband.

'His manner was decisive, but polite,' Jane read. She looked up at Robert.

Her voice was clear and she spoke her words carefully and read beautifully. Everyone admired Jane when she read her stories.

Outside the rectory Tom Lefroy was arriving late, as always. He pulled angrily at his long green coat as it became caught in some tall plants. Thoughts about being in London with his friends were in his mind.

When he stepped into the rectory, the door shut loudly behind him. In the sitting-room, everyone jumped.

Jane stopped reading.

'May I introduce my nephew, Mr Thomas Lefroy,' said the older Mr Lefroy, looking embarrassed.

'He is welcome,' said Mr Austen kindly.

Tom bowed politely to the room full of people, took off his coat and sat down next to John and Henry.

Lucy pulled Jane's arm and said quietly, 'What a handsome green coat. Those have become quite popular in London.'

John said to Tom, 'You will find this story very amusing.'

But Tom just smiled. Then he prepared himself to become bored.

Jane continued reading her romantic story. Everyone except Tom was enjoying it.

'There is writing on *both* sides of those pages?' he said quietly to John after a minute or two.

He preferred the excitement of London bars and clubs. He closed his eyes.

As Jane finished her story, everyone clapped. Only Tom showed no enjoyment. He was asleep.

John called out, 'Well done, Jane.'

Jane turned towards John and noticed Tom next to him. She saw Tom suddenly wake up and her face turned red. She felt like crying.

Later in the evening, as Jane talked to Cassandra and Robert about their plans for the future, she heard John and Tom Lefroy behind her.

She heard John say, 'What a wonderful story from a very clever girl.'

Jane smiled to herself, but her smile soon disappeared.

'I thought it was childish,' Tom replied. 'Not like the stories that we hear in the city. I cannot wait to return to London at the end of the summer.'

Jane held back her tears and walked out of the room. She moved as quickly as she could with her notebook in her hand. Then she ran up the stairs to her bedroom. There, she began to pull the pages out of her notebook, quietly crying. She threw them into the fire. Then she looked under her bed and found her box of notebooks. On the box she wrote the word 'childish'. She felt like a stupid child.

Chapter 5 In the Forest

A few days later, Tom's relatives went hunting. Tom did not know anything about guns or hunting, so he stayed at home. He missed his friends and his exciting life in London. Soon he was bored in the house and decided to take a walk.

He followed a path away from the house. After some time, he found himself walking in a beautiful forest of tall, thick trees.

Suddenly, he realised that he was not on the path. He turned around to return to the house. But he could not remember the way. To Tom, every path looked the same in the forest. He fell over some large stones. When he picked himself up, he found two paths going different ways. He did not know which one to take.

Jane was also walking in the forest, with her notebook. She was enjoying the silence of the forest and thinking about a new story. As she turned onto another path, she saw Tom Lefroy between the trees. She looked away from him.

But Tom saw Jane walking through the forest in front of him. It was strange that she did not say hello.

'Miss?' he called. 'I am lost.'

Jane moved faster along the path.

Tom started to run, calling again. Then he fell over a dead tree into a small pool of water. Jane looked quickly behind her and laughed to herself.

Tom got up and shook his coat. He spoke more loudly. 'Perhaps you could help me, Miss?'

Jane finally stopped and turned to him. 'Austen,' she said coldly.

'Mr Lefroy,' Tom said, bowing.

'Yes, I know,' said Jane quickly. 'But I am *alone*.'

'Except for me,' Tom said with a smile.

Jane said with a serious face, 'Exactly.'

Tom stepped closer to her and said, 'What are the rules in this situation? We were introduced a few nights ago. Can we not talk together in the forest now?'

'But you could not remember my name. You could not stay awake when we were in the same room.' Jane walked away again.

Tom did not know what to say. He bowed politely and started to walk along a different path.

But Jane was still angry with him. She turned to follow him.

'The situation in a forest may seem very simple, even *childish*, to a man from the city,' she said, speaking quickly.

'I am told that one can admire many things on a walk in the forest,' Tom said, not understanding. 'And I can see only green above and brown below.'

'Other people have noticed more than that,' Jane said. 'There is a book about this forest.'

'Oh,' Tom said. 'Do you mean fiction?'

'Ah, fiction! Stories are, of course, read only by women. Sometimes – and that is worse – they are *written* by women.'

'But *I* read fiction,' said Tom.

Jane was surprised. 'You do?'

'My favourite book is called *The History of Tom Jones*,' he continued. 'Perhaps you have read it?'

'I am afraid I have not,' Jane said quickly, wanting to end the conversation.

'That is no surprise,' he said. 'Your life has not taught you about those things. But there is a copy of the book in my relatives' library. I am sure you can borrow it from them.'

Jane thought for a few seconds and then asked, 'What do you mean by "those things"?'

'The story has many bad characters in it,' he said.

'I see,' she said, feeling again like a child.

'It is a wonderful story by a clever young man.'

'Some wonderful stories are written by clever women,' she said.

Tom finally understood. 'So we are talking about the story that you read a few nights ago,' he said. 'Did I not admire you enough?'

'You were asleep.'

Tom looked embarrassed. 'The story was ...' he began to say.

Jane turned and started to walk away.

'But if you want to write good fiction,' Tom added quickly, 'you need to know more about life.'

Jane stopped and turned around again.

'Do I?' she said coldly. 'And why should I listen to your opinion?'

'I know more of the world,' he said.

'You know more?' she asked.

He smiled at her and said playfully, 'I know enough. I know that you know little about it.'

Jane was embarrassed now. 'I must go,' she said quietly. She walked along the path more quickly.

Tom called after her, 'I hope I did not hurt your feelings.'

'Not at all,' Jane shouted. Then she hurried to get away from him.

'Oh, how do I get home?' he called.

She pointed to a path without speaking.

He watched her as she continued on her way. What an interesting young woman, he thought.

Chapter 6 A Night of Dancing

Eliza, Jane, Henry and John arrived together at the Basingstoke Dance.

The air was filled with excitement. Along the walls and around the windows of the large room were candles and flowers. At the back, there was another room with a long table of drinks and food.

Jane wore a pretty dress made by her mother. Her wavy hair was pulled up on top of her head.

'Mr Wisley has seen you,' Eliza said to her.

'From that height he can see most of the area,' Jane replied, turning her back to Mr Wisley.

Henry moved closer to Eliza and she quickly took his arm.

'How kind, Cousin,' she said.

She gave Jane a wide smile as Henry took her to the dance floor. Jane was left alone.

Suddenly, Mr Wisley stood in front of her. Jane smiled politely, but did not want to have a conversation with him.

'Miss Austen,' he said, 'may I request the next dance?'

Outside, Mr and Mrs Lefroy, their daughter Lucy and nephew Tom were just arriving. Lucy was very excited because this was her first time at the Basingstoke Dance.

As soon as they stepped into the main room, Tom's eyes searched for Jane. He saw that she was dancing with Mr Wisley.

Mr Wisley stepped on Jane's foot.

'Oh!' she cried.

'I am sorry,' Mr Wisley said. 'I do practise, but I cannot get better.'

After the dance, Jane tried to walk quickly to the other room to get a drink. This was not easy because her toes were still aching. With a drink in her hand, she joined Eliza, Henry and John. Tom watched her from across the room and slowly started to walk towards her.

Eliza asked Jane, 'What do you think of Mr Lefroy?'

Lucy joined the conversation. 'My cousin Tom? I think he is a very fine man. We are …'

'Pleased that he is here tonight,' Jane joked.

'Oh?' said Eliza.

'Well, he does have a silly green coat and bad manners,' Jane continued. 'He thinks he is so special.'

'Jane – ' Henry said quickly.

But Jane continued, 'And he refuses to dance when there are so few men here. It is a good thing that he is only here for a short time. Henry, are all your friends so unpleasant? Where in Ireland does he come from?'

From behind her Tom's voice said, 'Limerick, Miss Austen.'

He bowed.

Jane felt very embarrassed.

'The next dance is going to begin,' Tom said, holding his arm out to her.

She did not know what to say. So she took his arm and he walked her to the dance floor. As the dance began, Tom said, 'You are the first woman in Hampshire to dance with me.'

'Then your reputation in the country needs a good report from me,' she said with a smile.

Tom held her waist and they danced in a circle. They then stood opposite each other.

'This is a country dance,' Jane explained. 'It is what simple people in the country do.'

Tom laughed. 'Do you really think that?'

Jane replied, 'I was describing what you were thinking.'

'Please – I can think for myself,' Tom said as he took her arm. His wide eyes watched her turn around him.

'And I can think for *my*self, sir,' she said. 'Will you agree that a woman can?'

'Perhaps. But what does the woman think of me?' Tom asked as they continued to dance.

She answered, now holding his hand, 'That you are too important for the simple activities of the country.'

'And I think that you, Miss …' Tom started to say as he followed the dance. He then stepped to one side, still holding her hand.

'Austen,' Jane said with a smile on her face. 'Mr …?'

'Lefroy,' Tom said, smiling back at her. 'You think that you are better than other people.'

Jane stopped dancing and dropped his hand. She could not believe what she was hearing. She looked angrily at him.

'Me?' she asked.

'You, Miss Austen,' Tom said. 'Secretly,' he added.

'It is what simple people in the country do.'

Jane realised that her mother was watching them. She continued to dance, but did not say another word to Tom. Together, they moved smoothly across the dance floor. For the first time, Tom was enjoying life in the country.

Mr Wisley was also watching them until he looked away unhappily. Mrs Austen, noticing this, crossed the room to him. She quickly started talking to him about Jane.

When the evening ended, Jane and Eliza left together. Henry and John followed closely behind them.

'How many times did you dance with Tom?' Eliza asked Jane.

'Twice is fine,' Henry said. 'But three times and people will think you like him.'

Jane counted the dances on her fingers and realised her mistake.

Sounding like an older brother, Henry continued seriously, 'Be careful, Jane. Mr Lefroy does have a reputation.'

When Jane was finally alone in her bedroom, she took out a notebook. She put her pen into a bottle of ink and wrote quickly and angrily: *rude, unkind, unpleasant ...*

After she finished, she read her words again. 'Exactly,' she said to herself.

Feeling better, she went to bed. But she could not sleep, so she picked up the book at her bedside. It was Tom's favourite book, *The History of Tom Jones*.

Chapter 7 At the Country Fair

Every summer there was a country fair near the Austens' village in Hampshire, and this year was no different. The park was filled with people enjoying games and music. All around there was singing and laughing.

Jane, Eliza, Henry and John arrived at the fair as the sun was going down. At the gate they saw Tom and his young cousin Lucy. They greeted each other politely and continued to walk together into the park.

'The Leverton Fair!' Lucy said. 'I am so glad that you suggested coming, Jane.'

Tom and Jane looked at Lucy and smiled at each other. Then, they watched two colourfully dressed men throwing sticks of fire into the air. With wide eyes they saw the men catch the hot sticks in their hands.

Busy with their own conversation, Eliza and Henry walked away from the others.

'I see that you are not wearing your red soldier's coat,' Eliza said.

'My father thinks that a black coat is better for a future man of religion,' he replied.

'But a red coat suits your character better.'

Henry smiled at her. It was clear that she understood him.

Tom and Jane were stepping carefully across the wet ground when a drunken man fell down in front of them.

'A countryman, Miss Austen?' Tom said, jokingly.

Jane just smiled at him as they walked around the man. They were soon in a crowd who were watching two men boxing.

'Trouble here,' Jane said, not wanting to watch.

But Tom was interested. 'And excitement,' he said.

Jane looked away each time the larger man hit the smaller one.

'Only a stupid person boxes with a professional,' Tom said.

'You know about that, of course,' said Jane. She closed her eyes when she heard the man being hit. 'Perhaps it is very popular in London, watching men hurt each other.'

The smaller man was knocked to the ground. Tom quickly took off his coat and handed it to Jane.

Surprised, Jane said, 'Mr Lefroy! What are you doing?'

But it was too late. Tom was already stepping into the boxing area. He was ready to teach the boxer a lesson.

'Stop!' Jane cried.

Henry saw what was happening. He was not worried at all. He called out to the crowd, 'Five shillings* if the young man wins.' A few people were happy to put their money on the professional. Tom tried a few times but failed to hit the other boxer. The men danced around each other, Tom looking more and more angry. The other man hit the air and missed Tom.

John and Lucy joined the crowd. Lucy was surprised to see her cousin there. 'Tom! Wonderful!' she called.

Tom heard his cousin's voice and turned his head for a second. That proved to be a mistake. The other boxer hit poor Tom in the face, and he fell back hard on to the ground. He was clearly in pain.

Jane ran to him immediately, now very worried, and helped him to get up.

Henry was paying people their five shillings.

'You spend money too easily,' Eliza said.

Henry looked embarrassed. Then Eliza laughed, and he smiled.

As Tom put on his coat, Jane asked, 'Why did you do it?'

'I had all those expensive boxing lessons,' he replied, cleaning the blood from his nose.

'You fought because the last fight was unfair,' Jane said. 'I admire that.'

'Unfair?' Tom joked. 'I am a lawyer. There is no fairness in the law.'

♦

* shilling: a type of money used in Britain in the past

Later, at the rectory, Mrs Austen called Jane to her. She was not happy.

'Leverton Fair! At night! With Mr Lefroy!' she screamed, while Jane kept her head down.

'But Henry was there. And Eliza, John and Lucy too.'

'But Mr Wisley will hear about this,' her mother continued.

Jane looked up. 'Do you mean that he will not want to marry me?' she said coldly.

'That is not what I mean – '

'Then all is well,' Jane said. 'My price has not changed.'

She started to leave the room.

'Jane!' Mrs Austen called. 'You will not see Mr Lefroy again!'

As Jane walked away, her father joined his wife in the sitting-room. Jane stopped at the bottom of the stairs and listened to their conversation.

'At the end of the summer Mr Lefroy will be gone,' Mrs Austen said, sounding calmer now. 'And Mr Wisley will wait – I hope.'

Mr Austen shook his head. 'The man is so boring.'

'He will grow out of that,' his wife said. 'And she can change him. You should tell her.'

'Tell her what? To be unhappy?' said Mr Austen, 'Jane should have the man she wants.'

Still on the stairs, Jane smiled.

Chapter 8 Mr Wisley's Offer

It was a warm summer morning and Jane was sitting in the garden. She enjoyed the quiet mornings, writing in her notebook with the smell of flowers all around her. She was thinking about Tom Lefroy and she decided to write a new story. It was about a young woman who falls in love with the wrong man.

Mrs Austen, Lady Gresham and Mr Wisley came into the garden from the rectory. When Jane saw them, she hid behind some tall plants. But there was no escape.

'Jane, at last,' her mother said. 'Lady Gresham and Mr Wisley are visiting us.'

Jane greeted their guests politely.

Lady Gresham said, unsmiling, 'Of course, the young people will prefer to walk. I see that there is a pretty little garden here.'

Jane suddenly had an idea for her story and did not want to forget it.

'Excuse me,' she said, as she picked up her pen and bottle of ink. She then sat down to write in her notebook.

'What *is* she doing?' Lady Gresham asked.

'Writing,' Mr Wisley said simply.

'Can anything be done about it?' Lady Gresham asked.

But no one answered.

Soon Jane and Mr Wisley were walking together in the garden. Jane was very uncomfortable. She knew that he wanted to talk to her about her future.

'Miss Austen,' he said nervously. 'I have …'

'The garden is so beautiful in this season.'

Mr Wisley did not seem to be listening. He continued, 'I have known you for a long time now, and the feelings that I have –'

Again, Jane stopped him. 'And I like the flowers best at this time of year.'

'I own land in this country and in the West Indies,' Mr Wisley said. 'And one day, I believe, my aunt's land – '

'Sir, stop.' Jane tried again.

Mr Wisley went down on one knee and took Jane's hand. He spoke quickly. 'It is yours if we marry. All of it. Yours.'

'Mr Wisley,' Jane said coldly. 'Your offer is very kind, and you are a kind man. But I cannot accept. I cannot marry without ...' She stopped, looking embarrassed.

'Love.'

'Yes,' Jane said, surprised.

They looked at each other.

'Sometimes love is a shy flower,' Mr Wisley said. 'It takes time to grow.'

♦

Later that day, Jane was working in the Austens' vegetable garden when her mother came outside. At first they did not speak as they searched for potatoes. Mr Austen began working quietly in another part of the garden.

Finally Mrs Austen said, 'There is no money for you. We have very little, and that will go to your brothers. When we are gone, you will have nothing without a husband.'

Jane pulled a potato out of the ground and said, 'Then I will have nothing. I will not marry without love.'

'Do you really want to be poor, old and single?' her mother asked. 'You will be the subject of jokes in the village.'

Jane continued to work. She thought about what her mother was saying. It was all true. She started to cry quietly to herself.

'Love is very nice,' her mother continued. 'But money is necessary.'

'Perhaps I can live by writing,' Jane said softly.

'What? Don't be silly, girl!'

As Jane ran away angrily, Mr Austen stopped his work. He followed her to the other side of the house. Jane was feeding the pigs, pushing the tears from her face.

'He will give you a good home and a comfortable life,' her father said kindly.

Surprised, Jane said, 'Father!'

'This has been your only offer,' her father added.

'But Wisley?'

'It is true,' Mr Austen said. 'He is …'

'Boring.' Jane completed his sentence.

Her father said calmly, 'Yes, but he will probably grow out of that.' Jane watched as the pigs fought for the food. 'You don't want to be poor all your life.'

♦

A few days later, there was a big party at Lady Gresham's house. The front of the great house was brightly lit, and it looked like a palace. Jane arrived with her parents, Henry, John and Eliza. She was dressed in a beautiful soft green dress, but she did not feel beautiful. As she stepped into the large main room, she noticed the expensive furniture. Then her eyes grew wide when she saw some of the rich guests. They were wearing silver and gold, and expensive clothes.

Of course, Jane had to dance with Mr Wisley. She felt that it was her duty. But it was clear to everyone that she was bored. As they danced, he stepped on her foot again. She smiled politely, then looked at her mother. Mrs Austen was watching her very closely. When the dance finished, Jane quickly walked away.

She was suddenly greeted by Tom Lefroy. He held out his hand and they began the next dance together. They moved smoothly and happily across the dance floor, and she was not bored.

'You dance with feeling,' Tom said to her.

'No sensible woman should show her feelings,' Jane replied with a smile. 'She will never get a husband.'

Then she saw the look on her mother's face and her smile disappeared.

Tom knew that something was wrong. He held her closer as they danced. But she pulled back, knowing that she should not enjoy herself. He tried to hold her closer again. She wanted to be near him. But suddenly she stopped dancing.

'Excuse me. I am too warm and I need air,' she said softly.

As she started to walk away, he reached out to her.

'Wait,' he said.

But Jane continued to walk through the crowds of party guests until she was outside in the fresh night air.

She stood in the garden. It was dark, lit only by candles. She looked unhappily at the lakes and at the lines of trees.

Suddenly, she heard voices talking near her. At first she could not see who it was. Then, when she moved a little closer, she saw Henry and Eliza. They kissed and, surprised, Jane turned away. She did not know what to think.

As she walked back to the house, Lady Gresham came up to her. Jane bowed.

'Miss Austen,' Lady Gresham said, unsmiling, 'I cannot believe that I must have this conversation.'

Jane stood nervously and listened.

'Mr Wisley's mother, my dear sister, died young. I have no children, so my nephew is important to me. I will do anything to make him happy.'

'I understand, madam,' Jane said.

Lady Gresham's voice became angry. 'When a rich man like my nephew is interested in a young woman, she must accept immediately. But what do we find?'

'A young woman with her own ideas,' Jane answered nervously.

'Exactly!' Lady Gresham was displeased. 'Your family is admired because your father is a good rector. Also, of course, your cousin has a title. But your father does not have much money. Luckily for him, he has a daughter. This daughter can choose to become very rich.' She gave Jane a cold look, and returned inside to her guests.

Jane stood in the garden. She did not know what to do next. Then she heard Tom's voice behind her.

He said softly, 'I have heard that Mr Wisley has made you an offer of marriage. You should accept.'

They faced each other in silence. They both knew that their feelings were too strong.

Finally Jane said, 'Are you really leaving tomorrow?' Her eyes filled with tears. She stepped closer to him and kissed him. He held her for a few seconds and then kissed her. She did not want him to stop.

'I have no money,' Tom said. 'I am nothing without my uncle's money, and he will never agree to our marriage. So I cannot offer you marriage, Jane,' he continued. 'But you must know what I feel. I am yours. My heart is yours.'

She took his hand and they sat together in silence for a few minutes.

He finally spoke. 'What shall we do?'

'What we must,' Jane said.

Chapter 9 Eliza's Plan

The next day, Jane discussed her situation secretly with Henry and Eliza in the rectory garden.

'Shall I go to London? Perhaps I can do something there,' she said.

Eliza said, 'But you are an unmarried woman. You cannot travel alone.'

'Oh, help me, please,' Jane asked.

Henry and Eliza thought about it. Then Henry said, 'You are right, Jane. Perhaps you should visit Tom's uncle.'

'But how can I?'

Eliza looked at Henry, and they understood each other.

He held her for a few seconds and then kissed her.

'We can visit your brother Edward in Kent to help Cassandra,' Eliza suggested. 'The baby will be here soon. Of course, we must travel with a man – the right kind of man.'

Both women looked lovingly at Henry.

He said slowly, 'Perhaps we can stop in London on the way and visit the judge. He is a relative of our close neighbour.'

'A perfectly sensible idea,' Jane said with a laugh. She felt better now.

◆

A few days later, Jane, Henry and Eliza were in Judge Langlois's London home, being introduced by Tom Lefroy.

'Comtesse?' The judge asked, as he was introduced to Eliza. He was always pleased to meet an aristocrat. He smiled as he bowed to Eliza and her cousins.

That evening, they all had dinner together in the large dining-room. They discussed many interesting subjects. Henry told the judge about his time as a soldier. Eliza explained how she kept her money safe during the war in France. Jane was less of a success. His uncle's face as she seemed to joke about serious subjects worried Tom.

'My cousin, Jane, is a writer,' Eliza explained.

'Of what?' the judge asked.

Jane became very nervous. 'Fiction, sir,' she said quietly.

'A young woman from a good family?' the judge said, not believing her words.

Eliza and Henry smiled at Jane. There was an uncomfortable silence.

Jane noticed Tom's worried face across the large wooden table. 'There are women writers who make money,' Jane said.

'From writing?' the judge asked.

Tom felt he needed to help Jane. 'I know of a female writer who has made five hundred pounds from one book. She was given seven hundred pounds for her next book.'

The judge shook his head and finally smiled at Jane. 'You are a clever young lady, Jane, with many ideas. Perhaps one day you will succeed as a writer.' He stood up, saying, 'I will leave you young people now and see you again in the morning. Do enjoy your stay here.'

When the old man left the room, the others laughed. Everything was going well. It seemed that Judge Langlois liked Jane.

When the judge was asleep in his bed, Tom showed Jane to her room. Jane followed him up the stairs by candlelight as her wide eyes viewed the expensive paintings on the walls. She was very excited, but spoke softly.

'Will I really have this?' she asked Tom.

'What?' he said with a smile.

'You,' she said. 'This life with you.'

When they arrived at the top of the stairs, he stepped closer to her. 'Oh, yes,' he said.

He wanted to kiss her again, but she stepped back. She knew that they could be seen there.

He touched her soft, pale face and said, 'My uncle will be kind, I am sure.'

'Will you speak to him?' she asked.

'Tomorrow.'

They said good night and Jane went into her room, but she was too excited to sleep. She thought about Judge Langlois agreeing to her marriage with Tom. She imagined herself in the future, living happily with Tom in that great house. She imagined her mother being proud of her.

She began to write in her notebook, just names at first: Elizabeth Bennet, Mr Bingley ... Mr Darcy.

Chapter 10 A Big Problem

The next morning, the post arrived as Henry, Eliza and Jane waited for the judge in the sitting-room.

The judge came downstairs and went into the dining-room. He looked at his watch in surprise when he saw Tom waiting for him.

'Has the world gone crazy?' he said. He sat down and started looking at the letters.

As the judge ate his breakfast, Tom nervously began to speak. 'Sir, I would like to discuss something with you.'

'I cannot give you any more money,' the judge said, opening an envelope.

'I am pleased that you have met my friend Jane Austen,' Tom continued, as his uncle read the letter. 'I am sure you will agree with me. She is a fine young lady.'

The judge stood up angrily, his face becoming purple.

'This is terrible!' he said in a loud voice, waving the letter in the air.

Tom stepped back, frightened and surprised.

'This letter explains everything. You do not need to say anything more,' the judge said angrily.

'What letter?' Tom asked.

'Now I know exactly what the two of you were doing in Hampshire,' the older man said, throwing down the letter. 'Is it true that you have feelings for this young woman?'

'I wanted to introduce you to her first, Uncle,' Tom said, his voice shaking.

'But first you introduced me to her rich, aristocratic cousin,' the judge shouted. 'I understand your little game now.'

In the sitting-room, Henry, Eliza and Jane then heard the judge call Jane 'a poor little husband hunter'! Eliza and Jane had to stop Henry running into the dining-room.

'I wanted you to meet her. She is a wonderful, clever lady,' Tom said.

Jane stepped closer to the door to listen. Henry and Eliza watched her with worried faces.

'Sir, what about my happiness?' Tom continued.

'Happiness?!' Judge Langlois said angrily. 'You will not be happy in a marriage with a woman like that.'

There was nothing more to say. The judge left the room, not finishing his breakfast. As he passed Jane, outside the dining-room, he looked at her without a word.

'My uncle has refused. He does not want us to marry,' Tom said sadly. 'And without his agreement, I will not get any more money from him.'

Jane shook her head.

'The letter has done its work,' Tom continued.

'But who sent it? Lady Gresham?' Jane asked.

'Or perhaps her nephew.'

'We are just toys to them,' Jane said angrily. 'They think they can destroy our lives.' She started to cry.

'But now we have to do as we are told,' Tom said simply.

'No, we do not,' said Jane.

There was an uncomfortable silence. Finally, Tom took Jane's hand and looked into her tearful eyes.

'But I need my uncle's money,' he said seriously. 'I must do what is right. I must think of my family.'

'Tom! Is that all you have to say?'

He was unable to reply.

Jane turned around and left the house. Henry and Eliza followed her. As she walked away, Tom watched unhappily from the window.

Chapter 11 Back Home

On the way home from visiting her brother Edward and his wife, Jane sat silently in the coach next to Cassandra. The two sisters were glad to be together again. But at the same time they were sad. Robert was in the West Indies, and Jane's dream of a life with Tom was gone.

As the coach moved slowly in the rain, Henry and Eliza fell asleep on the seat facing the girls. Eliza's head rested on Henry's shoulder.

♦

On her first day back at the rectory, Jane tried to keep busy with housework. She was hanging up the wet clothes when her mother called her. She told her daughter to dress for a visit to Lady Gresham.

Jane and Mrs Austen bowed when they were shown into the old woman's sitting-room.

'What news?' asked Lady Gresham.

'My son and his wife have a new baby. Another girl,' said Mrs Austen proudly.

With a small smile Lady Gresham said, 'I hope she is well.' She looked at Jane for a minute or two, making the younger woman feel very uncomfortable. Finally, she continued, 'Miss Austen, will you and your family accept my invitation to eat here this evening?'

'Yes, Lady Gresham,' Jane said sadly, as her mother smiled proudly. 'Thank you.'

♦

That evening, in the heavy rain, a messenger rode through the forest on horseback to Lady Gresham's house.

The old woman was in her dining room with her many

guests. The Austens were all there, with Eliza, John and, of course, Mr Wisley.

There was loud conversation as almost everyone enjoyed Lady Gresham's food. Only Jane was quiet. She was still thinking about Tom and did not eat much. When John asked about her visit to her brother, she answered his questions quickly. Then she said no more. She was polite, but the sadness in her heart made even that difficult.

There was a sudden knock on the door, and the messenger arrived with an important message for Jane's father. The other guests stopped talking in surprise. Mr Austen took the note and opened it immediately. As he read, his face turned pale.

The other people around the table waited for him to speak, and finally he lifted his head and looked at Cassandra.

The message was from the West Indies, and it was the worst possible news. After a short but serious illness, quite soon after his arrival, Robert Fowle was dead.

The dinner ended immediately and the Austens returned home.

Jane, her mother and Eliza stayed with Cassandra. The heartbroken young woman cried through the night.

When Cassandra finally fell asleep, early the next morning, Jane left her sister's room. She went for a walk in the garden with her notebook. But she was too tired and too sad. She could not write. She continued walking into the forest. It was difficult not to think about Tom. How could he be so cold to her? How could he think only about his uncle's money?

Henry and Eliza followed Jane into the forest. When they reached her, Eliza pulled at Henry's arm.

'I have more bad news, Jane,' Henry said. 'It is about Tom Lefroy.'

'What?' asked Jane, but she did not really want to hear it.

'I could not keep this a secret from you. The village will

The heart-broken young woman cried through the night.

know soon, and someone will tell you,' her brother continued.

'He is going to get married,' Eliza said quickly.

Surprised, Jane said, 'I see. So soon?' She suddenly felt weak and in a soft voice asked, 'Who is she?'

'A rich young lady from Ireland,' Henry explained. 'There was an agreement between Judge Langlois and the girl's father.'

Jane started to laugh because the situation seemed silly to her. 'Does the young lady know about this?'

'He has not been kind to you, Jane,' Eliza said.

'Who – the uncle or the nephew?' Jane replied, walking away from them. She had to be alone.

♦

A few days later, Cassandra woke up to the sound of Jane writing at the table in their room. She watched her younger sister in silence, then said, 'A letter?'

'No,' Jane replied. 'Something that I began to write in London. It is a story about two young women who are better than their situations.'

'There are many of those.'

'And two young men who get more than they should. There are many of them too.'

'How does your story begin?' Cassandra asked.

'Badly,' said Jane.

'And then?'

'It gets worse. But with some amusing parts, I hope.'

Cassandra thought for a minute, then asked, 'How does it end?'

Jane did not yet know the ending, but she looked at the sadness on her sister's face and said, 'The women both have surprisingly happy endings.'

Cassandra smiled for the first time in days and asked, 'Wonderful marriages?'

'To very rich men,' her sister added.

'Oh, Jane,' Cassandra said. 'He was dead for weeks and I did not know.'

'How could you know?' Jane said. 'No one has ever felt more than you have for Robert. But you could not save him.'

♦

The next day, their neighbour Mrs Lefroy visited the Austens for tea. 'I am glad to see you looking better, Cassandra,' she said kindly.

'Thank you,' said Cassandra, looking embarrassed.

'Is there any news in your family, Mrs Lefroy?' asked Mr Austen politely.

'My nephew is staying with us,' she said, watching Jane's face. Jane looked away. 'Just for a few days on family business.'

John spoke bravely. 'His marriage, perhaps.'

'He is well, I hope?' Mr Austen asked politely.

'Well enough.'

'Nothing seems to make *him* unhappy,' John said, looking warmly at Jane.

'Perhaps he has changed,' Mrs Lefroy said, still looking at Jane. 'He is not the same person.'

Mrs Austen stood up suddenly. 'Someone is coming,' she said in surprise.

Jane jumped to her feet.

'It is Mr Wisley!' Mrs Austen said.

'Yes,' said Jane. 'I invited him.'

She walked out of the room and joined Mr Wisley in the garden.

'You asked me a question,' Jane said quickly before he could speak. 'I am ready to give you my answer. It is now a better answer.'

He bowed and smiled at her, and they continued to walk.

'But there is one thing ...' She had to ask, but did not know how. 'You are a good man, Mr Wisley.' She thought for a few seconds and added, 'So I do not understand why you wrote the letter.'

'What letter?' he asked. 'I know nothing about a letter.'

'Or was it your aunt, for you?' Jane asked. 'It does not matter. One way or another, we are all made stupid by love.'

'In time,' Mr Wisley said kindly, 'I hope you will again have a higher opinion of love.'

'I think not,' Jane said. She stopped walking and turned to Mr Wisley. 'I thank you for your offer of marriage. I accept. Good day.'

And then she bowed and walked away.

Mr Wisley watched her as she moved past the flowers and out of his view. His mouth hung open in complete surprise.

Chapter 12 Tom's Offer

The autumn days were shorter and colder. Jane wore a coat around her shoulders as she walked through the garden. She noticed that most flowers were already dead. She took out her notebook to describe the brownness of it all. Then she heard footsteps on the path.

It was Tom Lefroy.

At first, neither of them could speak. She noticed that he was not wearing his long green coat. He wore black and looked like a lawyer now. He searched her large brown eyes, hoping for a sign from her about her feelings.

'Miss Austen,' he finally said softly.

'Mr Lefroy,' Jane said, unsure of herself, but trying to be strong. 'I understand that you will soon be married. Tell me about the lady.'

Tom looked embarrassed. 'She is from Ireland,' he said quickly.

'Your own country. Excellent,' she said. 'I see that she does not like your green coat. What was it that won her? Was it your smiles or your pleasing manners?'

Tom did not say anything more at first. He took out a few letters from his coat pocket and finally said, 'I cannot do this. I came to offer you an explanation. God knows what you must think of me. I know what I think of myself.' He put the letters back in his pocket, shaking his head. Again he said, 'I cannot do this.'

He suddenly stepped up to her and started to kiss her. She tried to push him away, but he continued. She hit him on the chest and he finally pulled back.

Again he said, 'I cannot do this.'

'What?' she asked.

'This,' Tom said. 'Any of it. Anything that is not with you. I cannot live this lie.' He looked straight into her eyes and asked, 'Can you?'

Jane was too surprised by his words to speak. She could feel her heart in her chest. Turning away, she said, 'I think you should leave now.'

'Come with me,' he said. 'Run away with me.'

Jane looked into his eyes. 'Marriage?' she asked. 'But without the agreement of my family or yours?'

'That is what I am offering,' Tom replied. 'I am not going to worry about my uncle. We can go to London tomorrow. By Friday we can be in Scotland and be married.'

In Scotland, but not in England, weddings could take place immediately.

Jane grew angry. 'And leave everything!'

'Everything,' Tom said decisively. 'It is the only way we can be together.'

'Unthinkable!' she said.

Tom stepped closer to her, saying, 'We were meant to be together.'

'Impossible! Mr Lefroy – ' she started, but he stopped her with another kiss.

This time, she did not push him away. After a few seconds, she lifted her eyes up to him.

Worried, she said, 'My mother will kill me.'

♦

The next morning, Jane was up before her family. She quietly finished filling her suitcase. Then she wrote a note to Cassandra, stepped carefully to her sister's bed and placed the note on top of the covers. She studied Cassandra's sleeping face.

But as she walked quietly and slowly to the door, she heard Cassandra's voice behind her.

'You will lose everything,' her sister said. Surprised, Jane turned quickly. Cassandra continued, 'Family. Your place in the world. For what? A life of being poor? A child every year and no money to feed them?'

Jane did not want to listen. She hurried to the door.

'How will you write?' her sister asked coldly.

Jane stopped and thought for a few seconds. 'I do not know,' she said. 'But happiness is in my reach and I cannot stop myself.'

Cassandra jumped out of bed. 'There is no sense in this,' she said.

Jane said softly, 'Imagine being with your Robert again – even like this.'

The two sisters looked seriously at each other. Cassandra lowered her head.

'Please keep this a secret for now,' Jane said.

Cassandra watched as her younger sister opened the door.

'Wait!' she said suddenly. She quickly went to her cupboard, took out a box and gave some money and a silver ring to Jane. 'Now go – quickly,' she said.

With tears in their eyes, the sisters kissed goodbye.

Chapter 13 Running Away

The sun was coming up as Jane and Tom ran through the forest with their suitcases. At the end of the forest, they waited on a country road. Jane was cold and shaking. As Tom held her close, she felt warmer in his coat. They could not hide the worry on their faces.

Finally, the coach arrived. The horses shook their heads as the coachman threw their bags on top.

After Jane's suitcase was tied down, Tom asked her, 'Are you sure?'

'Yes,' she replied.

He helped her into the coach, and soon they were leaving Hampshire. From the window, Jane watched the hills and valleys of her years as a child moving past her. She was happy with Tom, but at the same time frightened about their future together.

'Hampshire,' Tom said to her. 'Your home.'

'It was,' Jane said simply.

Suddenly, the coach stopped, caught in the soft, wet ground. The coachman asked the passengers to get out. As Tom carried Jane to drier ground, she was already starting to feel like his wife.

The men were trying to push the coach. Before he joined them, Tom gave Jane his coat. As he did, the letters in his pocket fell out. Quickly, she reached for them before they fell into the dirty water.

She could not help noticing the first line of one of the letters, in an open envelope. It began:

'Dear Tom,

Thank you for the money that you sent. We really needed it …'

She thought for a minute, then took the letter out of its envelope and read it. Then she walked away.

At last, the coach was freed from the dirty water. Tom looked up and saw Jane walking into the forest. He ran to catch her.

'We are ready to go now,' he said.

She stopped and looked down, deep in thought.

Tom stepped closer to her. Placing his arm on her shoulder, he asked, 'Worried?'

But she did not reply. She just put her head on his chest. Her face was sad.

'Are you worried about your reputation?' he asked.

'No,' she replied. 'Yours.'

He looked at her without understanding. Then the coachman shouted to them.

'Quickly now. We are late.'

Tom took Jane's hand and together they returned to the coach. As the journey continued, Jane was silent. She looked out of the window, still deep in thought.

Tom wanted to ask what those thoughts were. But there were strangers in the coach, and he could not. This was not the place to talk about personal business.

About five hours later, they stopped at a bar to change horses. The coachman told everyone to be back at the coach in twenty minutes. The passengers climbed out of the coach, tired from the uncomfortable journey.

In the bar, people sat down and warmed themselves in front of the fire. Jane and Tom ordered hot drinks. Jane did not want to eat because she still had something on her mind. Tom waited for her to speak.

Finally, she took Tom's hand and asked him sadly, 'How many brothers and sisters have you got in Ireland?'

Tom waited a second before answering. 'Enough,' he said nervously. 'Why?'

She took the letters out of his coat pocket, saying, 'What are their names?'

He suddenly realised that she knew about his large family. He was unable to speak.

Jane continued, 'They clearly need you. This will destroy your reputation and your uncle will stop giving you money. You need his money for your family.'

'But I can *earn* money,' he said, afraid now.

'It will not be enough.'

He shook his head and told her, 'I will not earn a lot at first, but in time.'

'Not with an important judge as your enemy, a wife from a poor family, and your brothers and sisters waiting for food. No, my sweet, sweet friend,' she said sadly, 'we will all be poor and unhappy.'

She reached for her hat, but he quickly took her by the wrist.

'I will never give you up,' he said.

A coachman from another coach called, 'Anyone for Hampshire?'

Jane stood up.

Tom stood up too and shouted at the coachman, 'Wait, wait.' He turned back to Jane. 'Don't speak,' he said. 'Don't think. Do you love me?'

She did not want to answer, but finally said, 'Yes. But if our love destroys your family, it will destroy itself. It seems that we were not meant to be together.'

'That is not true,' he said, pulling her to him.

He kissed her, but she pulled away.

'Goodbye,' she said.

Chapter 14 Another Sunday in the Country

It was late in the day when Jane walked slowly out of the forest, returning to the rectory with her suitcase in her hand. She stopped for a minute in front of her family's home. Did everyone in her family – everyone in the village – know about her and Tom? She tried to be brave.

When Jane stepped into the sitting-room, no one was there. 'Hello?' she called.

John ran into the room. He was clearly happy to see her.

'Where is everyone?' she asked.

'Looking for you,' John said excitedly. 'Your family is trying to keep this a secret, but perhaps it is too late. Lucy has probably told everyone in Hampshire by now. Where is that man, Lefroy? When Henry sees him, he will kill him.'

'There is no need. And he will not find him,' Jane said.

'So what ... happened?'

'Nothing "happened",' Jane replied as she sat down at the piano.

'I see,' John said, walking nervously across the room. He looked out of the window, then moved back towards Jane. 'I may not be as handsome as Mr Lefroy,' he said, going down on one knee. 'But my feelings for you …'

Jane stopped him, 'Please – I have no hope of marriage at the present time.'

'Hope? But Jane,' he said softly, 'you cannot imagine ...'

'Are there no other women in Hampshire for you?' she said angrily, walking towards the door. But then she stopped, realising something. She turned back to John and said, 'It was you who wrote the letter to the judge.'

'I have always loved you, Jane,' he said sadly.

She gave him a cold and angry look. He stepped back and quickly left the room.

♦

The next day was a Sunday and Jane walked with her family to church. Everyone in the family was worried about what people were saying about Jane and Tom. As the Austens arrived at the church, Lady Gresham and her nephew were also passing. But they did not stop.

The old woman shouted, 'Mr Austen, I must tell you that I will not be in church today. Not if this young woman is going to be there.' Her narrow eyes looked angrily at Jane.

'Why not?' asked Mr Austen.

'Aunt, please,' Mr Wisley said.

'I believe your youngest daughter has been ... on a journey,' Lady Gresham said.

'Do you think travelling is a crime?' Jane asked politely.

'You took a journey without your parents' permission and with plans to marry a man. And that man was not the one she agreed to marry,' Lady Gresham said loudly.

'Who has told you that?' Jane asked.

'Mr John Warren has told us,' the old woman said. 'And he is a friend of your family.'

'Not now,' said Mr Austen bravely.

'And,' Lady Gresham continued, 'my nephew takes back his offer of marriage. He cannot be seen with someone like you.'

Mr Austen stood next to Jane and held her hand tightly. Her mother stepped closer and stood on the other side of her daughter.

At the same time, Mr Wisley bowed to his aunt. He then took Jane's arm and walked her away from the others.

'Wisley!' Lady Gresham called angrily.

He said softly to Jane, 'It seems you could not marry without love – or even with it. I admire you for that. And I agree with you. I cannot either. I always hoped to win your love one day. But I want to be loved for myself, not for my money.'

Jane was surprised and happy to hear this. 'So are we still friends?' she asked him.

'Of course we are,' Mr Wisley said with a smile.

'I am glad,' Jane said, as they continued to walk.

'And you will live by your pen?' he said. 'Will your stories have happy endings?'

'My characters will have – after a little trouble – all that they want, with a home, a family and great happiness.'

That afternoon, Jane continued working on the story of Elizabeth Bennet and Mr Darcy.

Chapter 15 Twenty Years Later

Jane was with Henry and his wife Eliza in a theatre in London, listening to music. Henry and Eliza had some grey hairs, but were still happy together. Jane looked younger than her age.

Suddenly, she realised that people were looking at her. When the song finished, everyone clapped the singer. Then they turned to Jane and continued clapping.

Henry said, 'You are becoming famous, Jane.'

Jane stood and bowed politely, first to the front and then behind her. When she turned around, she saw Tom sitting a few seats behind her. He was watching her with interest. He, too, was older. But she knew who he was.

She looked away. She did not want to talk to him after so many years.

After the show, Jane was greeted by many people who enjoyed

reading her books. They wanted to meet her, and she politely spoke to a few of them.

As she tried to get away from the crowd, a young woman came up to her.

'Are you Miss Jane Austen?' she asked. 'The writer of *Pride and Prejudice*?'

Jane smiled politely, then hurried to the door. But it was too late. She saw Tom coming towards her.

'Lefroy!' Henry called. The two old friends greeted each other.

Jane continued to walk away.

♦

Later that night, there was a dinner party at Henry and Eliza's house. Many guests were already there when a few latecomers arrived. One of them was Tom.

Jane turned to Eliza. 'I will never forgive Henry for inviting him here.'

'Yes, you will,' Eliza said, and she smiled. 'We always forgive him for everything.'

Tom and Henry shook hands and Henry said, 'My old friend. Late as ever.'

Tom bowed to Jane. 'Miss Austen,' he said. He was clearly as uncomfortable as she was in this situation.

'Mr Lefroy,' Jane said politely.

Tom continued, 'May I introduce you to one of your admirers – my daughter, Miss Lefroy? Miss *Jane* Lefroy.'

The young woman stepped shyly towards Jane. 'Miss Austen,' she said. 'It is wonderful to meet you.'

Jane looked at her and said, 'You have your father's eyes.'

'Will you read for us tonight, Miss Austen?' the younger woman asked excitedly.

'She never reads at parties,' Henry explained.

The young woman looked unhappy.

Jane Austen looked at Tom with a small smile and thought for a minute.

'Tonight will be different,' she said finally, 'because my new friend wants me to.'

She sat next to the young Miss Lefroy and started to read the story of *Pride and Prejudice*. The story of how Elizabeth Bennet learnt to love Mr Darcy, and became his wife.

◆

Tom Lefroy married a rich woman. He became a lawyer, sat in parliament and, many years later, became Ireland's most important judge.

Neither Jane Austen nor her sister Cassandra ever married. Jane completed six very successful books before dying at the age of forty-one.

ACTIVITIES

Before you read

1 Do you know any of Jane Austen's stories, from books or films? Discuss what you know about her work. Tell the stories.

2 Look at the Word List at the back of this book. Discuss how important these are to you:
  a being *admired*
  b doing your *duty*
  c having good *manners*
  d having a good *reputation*
  e accepting your *situation* in life

3 Look at the photographs from the film in this book. Which of these activities can you see in them? Are any of these activities done differently now?
  a writing
  b greeting
  c dancing
  d talking
  e crying
  f sleeping
  g sitting
  h eating

While you read

4 Who are they? Write the characters' names below.
  a She is twenty years old. ....
  b She is Jane's sister. ....
  c She is Jane's cousin. ....
  d He is going to marry Cassandra. ....
  e She wants to be a writer. ....
  f She lives next door to the Austens. ....

g	He is going to be very rich one day.	....
h	He is Jane's brother.	....
i	He is going to stay with the Austens.	....
j	He is going to be a lawyer.	....
k	His nephew needs his money.	....
l	He likes and admires Jane.	....

After you read

5 Discuss these questions.

   a What do Jane and her mother disagree about?

   b Why does Judge Langlois want to teach Tom a lesson?

   c Why do the Austens stand while Lady Gresham sits?

   d Why does Tom prefer life in the city?

   e What do you think that Mr Wisley wants to ask Jane?

   f What does Jane think of Mr Wisley?

6 Work with another student. What do you think Lady Gresham and Mr Wisley say to each other after the Austens' visit to Lady Gresham's house? Have this conversation.

Chapters 4–6

Before you read

7 What do you think is going to happen next to these people?

   a Jane

   b Tom

   c Mr Wisley

8 Discuss these questions.

   a How important was marriage in Jane Austen's time?

   b How have opinions about marriage changed?

   c What are your feelings about marriage (for you or other people)?

9 Who says these words? Who are they talking about?

a	likeable	....	....
b	clever	....	....
c	decisive, polite	....	....
d	clever	....	....
e	interesting	....	....
f	fine	....	....
g	unpleasant, rude, unkind		
		....	....

After you read

10 Answer these questions.

   a Why do Cassandra and Robert have to wait to get married?

   b How do people act when Jane is reading to the group?

   c Why does Jane throw her notebook into the fire?

   d Why does Jane walk away when she first sees Tom in the forest?

   e What do both Jane and Tom enjoy doing?

   f How has Tom's view of Jane changed?

11 Tom's favourite book is *The History of Tom Jones*.

   a Look on the Internet. Find the name of the writer. What is the story about? Why do you think that Jane hasn't read it?

   b Do you have a favourite book? Tell another student about it.

12 Discuss Jane's feelings about Tom. What does she dislike about him? What does she like about him?

Chapters 7–9

Before you read

13 Who do you think Jane should marry – Mr Wisley or Tom? Explain why you think this.

14 In these chapters you will read about a fair and a big dance. What are these activities like in your country today? Describe a fair and a dance that you have been to.

15 Who is speaking? Who are they speaking to?

    a 'A red coat suits your character better.'

        ....

    b 'You fought because the last fight was unfair.'

        ....

    c 'My price has not changed.'

        ....

    d 'The man is so boring.'

        ....

    e 'It is yours if we marry.'

        ....

    f 'Sometimes love is a shy flower.'

        ....

    g 'Love is very nice. But money is necessary.'

        ....

    h 'I will do anything to make him happy.'

        ....

    i 'I am yours. My heart is yours.'

        ....

    j 'Will I really have this?'

        ....

After you read

  16 Discuss the differences between the Austens' home and situation, and Lady Gresham's.

  17 Work with another student.

    a How do you think Henry feels about his father's plans for his future? Have this conversation between Henry and his father.

    b Have a conversation between Jane and her mother about Jane's feelings for Tom.

  18 Discuss how these people feel about Jane becoming a writer.

    a Mrs Austen

    b Judge Langlois

    c Lady Gresham

Chapters 10–12

Before you read

19 Discuss these questions.

    a Tom is going to speak to his uncle about Jane. What do you think Judge Langlois will say?

    b In general, what are the older people's opinions of the younger people in this story? What do they think that young people should do?

    c Mr Austen is going to receive an important message. What do you think it will be about?

While you read

20 What happens first? Number these sentences 1–6.

    a Jane accepts Mr Wisley's offer. .....

    b There is news about Robert Fowle. .....

    c Jane leaves home. .....

    d Judge Langlois reads a letter and is angry. .....

    e Jane learns about Tom's future with another woman. .....

    f Lady Gresham invites Jane and her family to dinner. .....

After you read

21 Answer these questions.

    a What reasons does Tom give for following his uncle's orders?

    b Why is Jane sad when she returns home?

    c Why does Jane accept Mr Wisley's offer?

    d Have Jane's feelings for Mr Wisley changed?

    e Why does Tom return to Jane?

    f Why does Cassandra help Jane to run away?

22 Who do you think wrote the letter to Judge Langlois? Discuss the possible writers and their reasons with other students, and then take a vote.

23 Do you agree with Jane's decision to run away? Why (not)?

Chapters 13–15

Before you read

24 How do you think the story will end for these people?

   a Jane

   b Tom

   c Cassandra

   d Eliza

   e Henry

25 How have the lives of women changed since Jane Austen's time? Are there ways in which they haven't changed?

While you read

26 Finish these sentences. Write one word in each sentence.

   a Jane and Tom leave Hampshire by ....

   b Jane reads a .... that was in Tom's coat.

   c She understands that he really needs his uncle's ....

   d When Jane returns home, only .... is there.

   e She learns that he, too, wants to .... her.

   f Lady Gresham is rude to the Austens, but Mr Wisley is still Jane's ....

   g Twenty years later, Jane has .... married.

   h She is a very famous ....

   i She learns that Tom has named his daughter ....

After you read

27 Look at your answers to activity 24 and at what really happened. Were you right?

28 Tom and Jane take a long journey in a coach. Describe this journey. How is it different from travelling today?

29 Discuss these questions. What do you think?

   a Does Jane make the right decision, to leave Tom?

   b How difficult is it for Jane to return alone to Hampshire?

   c Was it a good idea for John to write the letter to Judge Langlois?

    d Why does Mr Wisley not make another offer of marriage immediately?

    e Do you think that Lady Gresham will forgive her nephew for walking away from her outside the church? Why (not)?

    f In what ways does Tom finally accept his uncle's plans for him?

    g Do you think that Jane has a happy life? What is there, at the end, for her to be happy or sad about?

30 Work with another student. Have a conversation between Tom and his uncle, Judge Langlois, after Tom returns from running away.

31 Have you read the book, or seen a film, of *Pride and Prejudice*? If you have, discuss these questions.

    a Which characters in *Becoming Jane* are like characters in *Pride and Prejudice*? How are they different?

    b How are the endings of the two books different for the main characters?

Writing

32 Write the letter that was sent to Judge Langlois about Jane.

33 Imagine that you are Henry. You have just been to Leverton Fair. Write about your evening and your feelings for Eliza.

34 Imagine that you are Jane. Write to your sister Cassandra while she is away at Edward's house. Tell her your thoughts about Tom.

35 Write the message that Mr Austen receives about Robert Fowle.

36 Imagine that you are Tom. Write a letter to your uncle explaining why you have run away with Jane.

37 Imagine that you are Tom. Jane has just left you at the bar and is on her way back to Hampshire. Write about your feelings.

38 Imagine that you are Jane. You have just learnt that John wrote the letter to Judge Langlois. Write in your notebook what you think about John.

39 Imagine that you are going to write a story. It takes place at the time of this book. Write descriptions of the clothes worn by men and women in those days.

40 Which people in this story are most interested in money? Explain why they are interested. Describe their characters.

41 Twenty years pass between Chapters 14 and 15. What happens during that time to Tom and Jane? Write another short chapter.

WORD LIST

admire (v) to like someone because they are good or clever

aristocrat (n) a person with a title, which they usually have as result of their parents' position

bow (v) to lower your head when you greet someone

box (v) to fight someone with your hands

candle (n) something that burns slowly. As it burns, it gives light.

character (n) a person in a story; everything about a person that makes them different from other people

clap (v) to show your enjoyment by hitting your hands together with short, loud sounds

coach (n) a large vehicle pulled by horses

duty (n) something that you have to do

each other (pron) words used when each person does something to the other

embarrassed (adj) feeling shy and uncomfortable

fair (n) an outdoor party or market with games

hunt (v) to catch animals and kill them

ink (n) coloured liquid that you put a pen in before writing

lawyer (n) a person who gives people information about the law

manner (n) a way of doing something. **Manners** are polite ways of acting

nephew (n) the son of your brother or sister

rector (n) a person with a job in the Church of England who is important in an area. A **rectory** is the rector's home.

reputation (n) the opinion that people have about someone

situation (n) the position that a person is in – in their life, for example, or at that time and in that place